FUN FOR THE
SECRET SEVEN

Brownie and Scamper tearing over the lawn (pg 84)

Enid Blyton's
Fun for The Secret Seven

Illustrated by Dorothy Hamilton

AWARD PUBLICATIONS LIMITED

ISBN 0-86163-536-1

Text copyright © Darrell Waters Limited
Illustrations copyright © 1991 Award Publications Limited

Enid Blyton's signature is a trademark of Darrell Waters Limited

First published 1963 by Hodder and Stoughton

This edition first published by
Award Publications Limited, Spring House,
Spring Place, Kentish Town, London NW5 3BH

Photoset by Rowland Phototypesetting Limited
Bury St Edmunds, Suffolk

Printed in Hungary

Contents

One

A meeting, please!

'PETER! Peter, where are you?' shouted Janet, racing up the stairs.

'Here – in my room,' called Peter, appearing at his door and looking very cross. 'I'm tidying it up. Dad looked in this morning, and wanted to know if I *liked* living in a pigsty! He said the pigs were tidier than I am!'

'Well – he was about right,' said Janet, looking round the room. 'Do you *ever* pick anything up when you drop it? Goodness, what's this mess on the carpet – something stuck to it?'

'Oh – so *that's* where my nougat went!' said Peter, scraping a sticky mess off the carpet. 'Good thing Dad didn't tread on that – it would have stuck to his shoe for ages!'

Janet gave a delighted chuckle. 'You really are dreadfully untidy, Peter,' she said. 'I suppose I'd better tidy up your room for you before Daddy comes back again.'

'What did you want me for?' asked Peter, still scraping. 'Ooh – it's horrid, this. What a waste of a nice bar of nougat.'

'Listen, Peter – a note came through the letter-box just now. It's addressed to "Peter, Head of the Secret Seven." So it's for you. Who is it from, do you suppose?'

'Oh, one of the others wants something, I expect. Maybe a meeting of the Seven for some reason,' said Peter, tearing open the envelope. 'Yes – it's from Jack. Listen. He says:

Dear Peter,

Will you call a meeting? I have had a strange request for help from Bob Smith. He's in our form at school, you know. He didn't say much except that he needs our help badly. He's pretty upset. Perhaps the Secret Seven can help him – he's a decent little fellow. Anyway – isn't it about time we met again, before we all forget we're the Secret Seven?

Jack

'Oh dear!' said Janet. 'He sounds rather high and mighty, doesn't he? I suppose you ought to call the meetings more often, Peter. They're great fun.'

'Well, after all, so many of us go away during the

summer holidays, it's hardly *worth* holding meetings then,' said Peter, rather red in the face. 'I wonder what's up with Bob Smith – and why he wants *our* help.'

'We've only got a week or so before the autumn term begins,' said Janet. 'You'll have to be quick about the meeting if we want to get all the members there.'

'Right,' said Peter. 'I'll scribble three notices of our next meeting, and you scribble two, Janet.'

So up they went to the playroom, and when Mother looked in to see why in the world they were both so quiet, she found them busily writing out the notes. She looked over Peter's shoulder, and read what he had written.

> *Please come to a meeting in the shed at half past two this afternoon. No one admitted without the password. We have to discuss something important. Bob Smith will be at the meeting. I shall ask him five minutes later than anyone else, in case he overhears the password. Wear your badge else you won't be allowed in.*
>
> *Peter*

'Well!' said Mother, in surprise. 'Whatever does Bob Smith want help for? I think . . .'

'Oh, Mother – you shouldn't have read that bit,' said Janet. 'It might be something secret. It *will* be fun to have another meeting! Peter – do you remember the password?'

'Of course!' said Peter. 'But I bet *you* don't.'

'No – I don't,' said Janet. She grinned at Peter's solemn face. 'It's all right. I've written it down in my diary, so all I have to do is to look it up. Ha! Ha!

You were sure I'd forgotten it. *You* tell me what it is
– I bet you don't remember, either!'

'Yes, I do,' said Peter, crossly. 'As if the head of
the Secret Seven could forget his own password! It's
Scamper's name – just "Scamper". Easy!'

'Thanks!' said Janet, with a grin. 'Now I shan't
have to look it up. Lovely password – Scamper!'

'Wuff!' said a surprised voice, and Scamper
raised his head from the floor, where he had been
lying waiting for the others to take him for a walk.
He leapt up and ran to Peter, putting his lovely
golden head on the boy's knee. Peter patted the
soft, silky head. 'You coming to the meeting too,
Scamper? All right. Half past two sharp. So don't
go rabbiting after dinner, because you won't be let
into the meeting-shed if you're late!'

Scamper gave a small whine, and licked Peter's
hand. How *could* he be late when he was going with
the two children?

'Did you remember to tell Jack in your note that
he could bring Bob Smith to the meeting?' asked
Janet.

'Yes. But he's to tell Bob to come five minutes
after us, so that he doesn't hear the password, and
so that we can ask Jack what's up with Bob, before
we see him,' said Peter, folding up the last of his

11

notes. 'Come on, now – we must deliver these at once, so that the others have plenty of notice about the meeting.'

They were soon on their way and went the round of Peterswood, popping the notes into various letterboxes. 'I do hope everyone will be able to come!' said Janet. 'Shall we take something to eat and drink? It's much more fun then.'

'Yes. Mother will help with that,' said Peter. 'I'll buy some sweets too. Luckily I've got some pocket-money left.'

'Well, NOT nougat, then,' said Janet, firmly. 'Even Scamper is tired of licking up dropped pieces. Buy some boiled sweets. They take ages to suck, and everyone likes them. Oh, I *am* glad we're to be the Secret Seven again! Come on, Scamper! We haven't finished yet!'

It wasn't long before all the notes had been delivered. They caused quite a bit of excitement. As soon as one had been dropped into Jack's letter-box and he had run to pick it up, he read it and raced after the two children going out of his front gate.

'Hey! I say! Are we *really* going to have a Secret Seven meeting this afternoon? Three cheers! I thought the Secret Seven had packed up!'

'Then you were an idiot,' said Peter, 'As soon as I

had your note I arranged a meeting at once. We're all back from holiday now, and it will be fun. Bring Bob Smith with you, as I said in my letter. We'll try to help him if we can.'

'I don't really know what's up,' said Jack. 'He didn't tell me. But I do know he's been going around looking pretty miserable. I bet we *can* help him!'

'See you at the meeting, then,' said Peter. 'I suppose you've lost your badge as usual?'

'I have *not*!' said Jack, indignantly. 'Just because I lost it once, you think I'm going to lose it always! And *I* didn't lose it then; my sister Susie took it, as you very well know.'

'Well, don't shout at me,' said Peter, grinning, 'else that awful sister of yours will hear you and try to come to the meeting with Binkie, that silly, giggly, twitchy-nosed friend of hers.'

'They're both going to a party,' said Jack, thankfully. 'So they'll be well out of the way. I do wonder what old Bob wants to tell us, don't you?'

'Well, we'll soon find out,' said Peter. 'By the way, Bob is to wait outside till we're ready to have him in. I put that in the note. Leave him some way off so that he can't hear what our password is.'

'Right,' said Jack. 'I've got the password written

on the back of the calendar in my room. It's . . .'

'Well, don't shout it out, or Scamper will come rushing to you!' said Peter, with a chuckle. 'So long, Jack!'

When Peter and Janet had delivered all the notes, and had a little talk with each delighted member, they went home, *just* in time for dinner! The gong sounded as they went in at the garden door.

'Wash your hands, quick!' said Janet. 'I'll wash mine with you to save time. Put the bottle of boiled sweets where we can see them in case we forget them. All right, Mother – we're coming! JUST coming!'

Scamper raced into the dining-room with them, hungry as a hunter. Where was his bowl of meat? Ah, there it was. Good old Mrs Simmons, she had got him JUST the kind of meat he liked best. Soon he and the two children were all eating hungrily. Mother laughed.

'Anyone would think that you two and Scamper hadn't had a meal for weeks!' she said. 'Scamper – don't gobble so. You'll choke! There – I knew you would!'

However, Scamper went on gobbling and had finished his dinner almost before the children had eaten three mouthfuls. He went to his rug and lay down, yawning. Ah – that was good! He wouldn't mind eating another whole plateful! He thought it was a pity that nobody ever offered him a second helping. He shut his eyes sleepily.

'Hey – don't you fall asleep, Scamper! You have to come to a Secret Seven meeting after we've finished dinner,' called Peter.

'Woof!' said Scamper, sleepily. He shut one eye and kept the other open.

'Funny to be half asleep and half awake like that,' said Janet. 'What's in that package over there, Mother?'

'Just a few new-made buns for the hungry Secret Seven!' said Mother, smiling. 'I made them this morning.'

'Mother, you're a great,' said Janet, and gave her a hug. 'I don't know why food tastes so nice when we all sit in the shed and talk. But it does.'

'I've some boiled sweets too,' Peter told his mother. 'And I dare say one or two of the others will bring something. Gosh – it *will* be fun to have a meeting again.'

At a quarter past two Peter and Janet left the house with Scamper, and went down to the meeting-shed. They carried the buns, the sweets, and four bottles of ginger beer.

'Let's hope one of the others brings something to drink too,' said Peter. 'Four bottles of fizz won't go far between seven of us on this hot afternoon.'

'Eight, you mean. Bob will be there,' said Janet. 'Nine, with Scamper!'

'Woof!' said Scamper, agreeing, his tail wagging hard.

Nobody had yet arrived at the shed. There it stood, the letters S.S. on the door. Janet pushed it open and looked inside. The shed was quite tidy, but it needed a dusting. She took the duster from a shelf and flicked it round the seats and little table. She put the bottle of sweets and the ginger beer on the table, and looked to see if the plastic mugs on the shelf were clean. What fun it was to be welcoming the Secret Seven members once more!

A knock came on the door and Peter spoke at once. 'Password, please.'

'Scamper,' said the voice, in a low tone. And then other footsteps came and low voices spoke the password, 'Scamper! Scamper! Scamper! Scamper!'

Scamper the spaniel was delighted to hear his name so often. He began to bark loudly, and leapt excitedly up at everyone as they came in.

'Sit, Scamper! I shan't use your name for a

password again if you get so excited,' said Peter. 'Anyone would think *you* were the head of this meeting, not me! Sit!'

Scamper sat, his tail wagging beneath him. Oh, how good to see all the Seven again – Colin – Pam – Barbara – George – and Jack – and Peter and Janet, of course.

Jack had come in alone, leaving his friend Bob outside as he had been told. They all sat down, and Peter sat on the stool at the head of the little table.

'Welcome!' he said. 'I'm glad you all remembered the password, and said it quietly. Now, Jack – will you please tell us exactly why you have called this meeting? But first call in Bob – he'll have plenty to tell us!'

Two

Bob Smith's story

THE Secret Seven meeting was soon under way. Jack stood up to tell everyone why he had wanted it called that afternoon. He looked worried, and spoke earnestly.

'Thanks awfully, Peter, for calling a meeting so quickly. You see, it's on account of something Bob told me. I saw him looking pretty worried yesterday and I asked him what was the matter and he told me about Old Man Tolly.'

'Old Man Tolly? The old fellow who lives in that tumbledown house on the top of the hill?' asked Peter, in surprise. 'What's the matter with him? *You* tell us all about it, Bob!'

'Well – he lives all alone except for an old horse and his dog,' said Bob. 'You've often seen that nice old horse – brown and white, with a lovely mane. Tolly's cottage has two rooms, and he lives in one, and Brownie the horse lives in the other.'

'Goodness – how odd!' said Pam.

'Not really,' said Bob. 'He loves that old horse. When old Tolly worked for the farmer on the hill beyond, he and the horse were together all the time. The horse was strong then, and could pull carts and wagons and goodness knows what. Then one day it pulled a heavy cart-load of stones down that big hill – and the weight made the cart run too quickly for the old horse, and it ran into his back legs and lamed them. So he wasn't any use for heavy work any more.'

'What happened then?' asked Peter.

'Well – the farmer blamed Tolly for the accident,' said Bob, 'and he said the horse was only fit to be shot, *he* wasn't going to buy fodder for him, if he couldn't work for his keep.'

'Oh! How DREADFUL!' said Pam and Janet together, tears coming suddenly into their eyes. 'Poor old horse!'

'Well, Tolly was heart-broken,' said Bob. 'He was sure that the horse-doctor – that vet man called Whistler – could make the horse's legs right again, and he called him in.'

'Good for him!' said Peter, and the others nodded.

'Well, it might have been good for the vet, but it wasn't very good for old Tolly,' said Bob. 'The

farmer wouldn't pay the vet's fees, though the horse was his, and told him to send the bills to *Tolly* – and they came to over fifty pounds!'

'Goodness!' said Peter, startled. 'What a lot of money! Surely Tolly couldn't pay all that?'

'Of course he couldn't pay all that!'

'Of course he couldn't,' said Bob. 'Apart from his pension, his wages are so low – he's old, you see, and can only potter about, and now he's really ill with worry. I was up there yesterday – my mother sent me up with some eggs – he used to work for us once, and we're fond of him . . . And he told me all about it then. He showed me the vet's bills too. Whew! I do think the vet might have kept his fees low.'

'My father won't use that new vet,' said Peter. 'He says he's too young and too hard. He hasn't learnt to love animals properly yet. He wouldn't even come to one of our cows one night when it got caught in a fallen tree. Poor thing, the tree had fallen on top of it in a high wind, and it was scared stiff, and one of its horns was broken.'

'Will he have old Tolly sent to prison if he can't pay?' asked Pam, in a frightened voice.

There was a shocked silence as the children thought of poor old Tolly all alone in prison, without the dog he loved, and without the horse whose friend he was.

'Have you come to us for advice?' asked Peter, at last. 'Is there something you want us to do?'

'Well – I simply don't know what *I* can do to help, and I thought you Secret Seven might have some ideas,' said Bob, looking round at them all, his face very worried indeed. 'How can old Tolly pay that bill? Where can he put the old horse now, so that the farmer won't take him away? I'm no good at solving puzzles like these – but I thought you Secret Seven could help somehow.'

There was a little silence, and then Janet spoke up, her eyes bright. 'Well, to begin with, I'm willing to empty my money-box to help to pay the vet's fees. Then that farmer won't have to worry about those, the mean old thing!'

Everyone began to talk at once.

'Yes, that's the first thing to do – pay the bill!'

'No! *I* think the first thing to do is to find some-where to keep the old horse safely. Don't let's have him left anywhere near that horrid farmer!' That was Pam speaking, very, very fiercely!

'Yes – Pam's right,' said Peter, knocking on the little table for silence. 'Pam's absolutely right. We *must* get the old horse out of that farmer's reach if possible.'

'Well, that would be easy – if we knew anywhere he could live,' said George. 'He's a big horse – I know him. He would need a decent stable, not a tiny shed.'

'Peter – wouldn't Dad let us have a place in one of our stables?' said Janet. 'Just for the time being, anyway. Dad wouldn't charge a penny, I know!'

'That's a good idea of yours, Janet,' said Peter. 'But remember, if we take that old horse away and stable him somewhere here, that horrid farmer may come after us, and charge us with stealing the horse!'

'Oh my goodness!' said Pam, scared. 'What can we do then? We've simply *got* to do something!'

'Well – we could find out how much the farmer wants for the old horse, and see if we can possibly earn enough money ourselves to pay for him,' said George. 'We've all got money-boxes. And if we hadn't enough, we could jolly well earn some more. What's the use of the Secret Seven if they can't tackle a thing like this?'

Bob flushed red with excitement. He stood up and spoke earnestly to the meeting. 'I KNEW the Secret Seven would do something. I KNEW they

would. I think you're great. Well – I really can't
TELL you what I think!'

'That's all right, Bob,' said Peter, kindly. 'We are
all glad you came to us about this. We'll do SOME-
THING, you may be sure – with your help too, of
course. You can't be a member of the Secret Seven,
but you can certainly be a helper with us, in whatever we do about this problem.'

Peter then addressed the meeting. 'I shall ask my
father to let us have a stall in one of the old stables.
Bob, will you please find out from Mr Tolly exactly
how much the vet's bills are – there may be more than
one – and if possible *get* the bills – and we could ask
the vet if he would be generous enough to take some
of the fees off, so that there won't be so much to pay.'

'Well – whatever the bills come to, even if the vet
reduces them, old *Tolly* can't pay,' said Bob. 'He's
only got his pension – his work is just a few jobs here
and there for the odd pound.'

'We want someone to clear up our orchard,' said
George. 'I'll ask Dad to get old Tolly, and pay him.'

Ideas came thick and fast, and everyone was
sorry when a knock came at the door, and Peter's
mother put in her head. 'I'm afraid the meeting
must soon stop. It's getting quite late!'

'Right, Mother,' said Peter, and waited till his

mother had gone. 'Now listen, everyone. This needs a lot of thinking about – a lot of considering. I am now going to close the meeting, and everyone is to go home, and think HARD this evening to get some kind of good idea about this problem. Come back here tomorrow morning at ten – you too, Bob – and we will sort out all our ideas and decide exactly what the Secret Seven can do to help – decide the BEST way to help. Tonight I shall ask my father about a shed or a place in our stable. That's the most important thing at present.'

'Oh, thank you, Peter,' said Bob, his face red with delight. 'I shan't worry tonight. I know you'll all think of something super by tomorrow. I wish I had your brains.'

'You've got something better, Bob,' said Pam, unexpectedly. 'You've got a VERY kind heart!'

And then out came the new buns and the fizzy ginger beer. Out came the boiled sweets and some chocolate and biscuits brought by Jack and Pam. What a feast!

When the little feast was over, the meeting broke up, and everyone went their way. They certainly had something to think about that night – something very difficult – something that had to be dealt with at once.

Three

Plenty of ideas

AT exactly ten o'clock the next morning there came a number of raps on the Secret Seven shed-door. The password, which was still 'Scamper', was whispered through the door and Scamper, who was inside with Peter and Janet, cocked his ears with pleasure every time he heard his name. He gave little whimpers of delight as the Seven filed in and took their places.

Last of all came Bob, out of breath with running. 'Had to do a job for my father,' he panted. 'Hope I'm not late.'

'We wouldn't have started without you,' said Peter. 'It's important that everyone should be here. Now, the meeting will begin. Stop chattering, please, Pam and Barbara.'

The two girls stopped at once, and faced Peter. This would be a worthwhile and exciting meeting, and they didn't want to miss a word!

'The meeting has now begun,' said Peter. 'Please

address any remarks to me, because if we all start chattering to one another, we won't get anywhere. First of all, I must tell you that Janet and I have asked our father about a place in one of our stables for Mr Tolly's horse.'

'He said yes,' began Janet, eagerly, and stopped as Peter spoke to her sternly.

'Janet! *I* was speaking!' said Peter. 'Please let me finish.'

'Sorry,' said Janet, going red.

'I'm very pleased to say that my father was sorry for Mr Tolly, and said that the farmer who owns the land on the hill was very hard-hearted,' said Peter, and everyone nodded in agreement.

'He said he would willingly give us a place in our biggest stable for Mr Tolly's horse – and he wouldn't charge him anything. BUT – he said he thought that Janet and I might like to keep the stable clean ourselves, so that the stable man wouldn't have to do any more work than usual.'

'I'll take my turn at that!' said George. 'No reason why you and Janet should have to muck it out all the time. I'd be pleased to come every Saturday.'

'Look – we'll *all* take turns,' said Colin. 'All of us. Why not? We've taken this thing on together, and we'll jolly well all share in everything. I'll come each Monday after tea.'

'And I'll come whenever I can,' said Bob. 'I must take my share. I'd like to – if the Secret Seven don't mind me butting in.'

'I think we'd better make you a temporary member,' said Peter, and the others nodded at once in agreement. Peter solemnly knocked on the table.

'I propose that we make Bob Smith a temporary member, until the matter he has brought to us is well and truly settled,' he said, in a very grown-up voice. 'Does the meeting agree to this proposal?'

Everyone agreed very loudly indeed. 'And now,' said Peter, 'I'd like to hear whether Bob has found out exactly what amount the vet's bill is.'

Everyone looked so solemnly at Bob that he felt he must stand up. He looked round at the others, feeling just a little wobbly on his legs. 'Er – thank you very much for saying that I can be a temper – tempory – well whatever it is – member. It's jolly kind of you. Yes, I did go and find out about the vet's bill. I went to Mr Whistler and I just asked him straight out how much old Mr Tolly owed him.'

'What did he say?' asked Peter.

'Well – he looked a bit startled, and asked me why I wanted to know,' said Bob. 'And I told him we were sorry for Mr Tolly, because he was afraid the horse would be shot if the bills weren't paid – and that we would do our best to get at least *some* of the money pretty soon, if he would wait.'

Bob paused for breath and everyone looked anxiously at him. What had the vet said?

'Well, the vet was jolly decent. He said that he hadn't understood that Mr Tolly would have to pay – and he said he would reduce the bill by half – and that I was to tell Mr Tolly he wasn't to worry, and that he'd still go on coming to see the horse and how it was getting on – and not charge him a penny more!'

'That was marvellous of him!' said Janet, her face one big smile. 'Did you tell him *we* would pay the bill ourselves, if he'd let us have time to earn the money?'

'Yes, I did, and he looked so astonished that I was sure he didn't believe me. He asked me what on earth we thought we could do to earn so much money. Even if he halved his bill, there would still be nearly forty pounds to pay. He said that Brownie's legs had needed daily attention for some time, and that was why his fees had mounted up. Actually they came to seventy-eight – and half that would be thirty-nine pounds fifty pence!'

'What did you say?' asked Peter.

'I just said that we'd talk it all over at our next Secret Seven meeting, and I'd let him know. I didn't like to make big promises on my own,' said Bob. 'But I did ask him if there was anything *he* wanted done, which one of *us* might be able to do.'

'*Was* there anything?' asked Colin, eagerly.

'Yes. He said his delivery boy – you know, Fred, who delivers any medicines for animals that the vet has seen during the day – well, he said Fred wanted two weeks' holiday to go and stay with his grandfather, and if any of us would like to do his rounds each evening, he'd pay him the same as he pays Fred.'

'How much is that?' demanded three or four voices at once.

'He pays him seventy-five pence a night,' said Bob. 'So I said *I'd* take Fred's place while he was away. You see, if I earn seventy-five pence a night for a whole fortnight – let's see, that's fourteen evenings at seventy-five pence a time – er – er – that would be . . .'

'You're no good at figures, Bob!' said Jack. 'You would earn exactly ten pounds fifty pence – and let me tell you, that's a lot of money! It would probably pay over a quarter of the vet's bill – gosh, this *is* a bit of luck, your getting the errand boy's job for a fortnight. If you get tired of it, one or other of us will take over for you.'

'I shan't get tired of it,' said Bob. 'The only thing is, I have to have one evening off a week to go to choir practice, so one of you can take over then.'

'Right. I'll do that evening for you this week,' said Peter. 'My word – fancy being able to knock off over a quarter of the vet's bill like this! Good for you, Bob. You did well.'

Bob sat down, his face flushed with pride. He decided to be the best errand boy that the vet had ever had. He decided to ask him if he could clean out the kennels in which the vet kept dogs when they were boarded out with him. That would be more money earned, perhaps. And would the vet like him to feed the cats each morning – or . . . Bob's mind ran on and on, and when he finally came to the end of his thoughts about the vet's jobs, he felt almost like a vet himself!

Yes – it was fun to be one of the Secret Seven – or was it the Secret Eight now? Bob made up his mind to be the best member they had ever had. His heart swelled with pride. A member of the Secret Seven – and the vet's errand-boy too – he really was getting on in the world!

Four

Mr Tolly – Brownie – and Codger

IN bed that night Peter thought about the successful meeting the Secret Seven had had that day. He and Janet were to clean out the stables in return for shelter for Mr Tolly's horse. The others would do their share of stable-cleaning too. Bob was to be an errand-boy – and they could take turns with him, if he wished. There must also be quite a bit of money in the money-boxes belonging to the Secret Seven. That would help to pay for fodder for Mr Tolly's horse. He would need something more than grass to eat . . .

Peter's thoughts grew muddled, and he found himself drifting off to sleep. He was happy. His worries about Mr Tolly and his horse began to fade, and his eyes closed in sleep. His last thoughts were of money-boxes – he must tell the members to open – their – to open their – money-boxes. Yes, their money-boxes! And then, with his thoughts getting all twisted up, he slid into dreams – strange dreams in which Mr Tolly, dressed as a little horse, ran about delivering medicine bottles to all the cows in his father's field!

Next morning Peter and Janet set off with Scamper to find Mr Tolly in his little tumbledown cottage on the side of the hill. He must be told the good news – that the Secret Seven were going to earn money to pay Mr Whistler's bills. Then he wouldn't worry any more about having to sell his brown and white horse.

There was the little cottage, whitewashed, leaning against the hill. Down in the valley below were flocks of sheep, every nose touching the grass in the meadow as they fed. Playing round them was Codger, a nice but ugly little mongrel dog, who thought his master was the finest man he had ever seen!

'Mr Tolly isn't with the sheep,' said Janet, looking down the hill. 'He must still be in his cottage. Let's go and see.'

As soon as the little mongrel dog saw the children going towards his master's cottage, he came tearing up the hill at top speed, barking fiercely. Who was this, DARING to go to his master's house? He barked round their ankles, and Janet was a little scared.

'Don't take any notice of his barking,' said Peter.

'He's only behaving like a good little watchdog. Come on, little dog – take us to your master!'

Tolly wasn't in his cottage. The children knocked and knocked, and finally tried the door. It opened. They peeped inside. The cottage was trim and neat and clean. Old Tolly couldn't keep it like that himself, surely! They went round to the back, where there was a small garden with a vegetable plot, and a washing-line. Taking down a sheet was a thin little woman.

'Hello!' said Peter, surprised to see a woman there. 'Is Mr Tolly in?'

'No, he's gone to do his shopping,' said the little woman. 'Look, isn't that him coming up the hill? Run and take that heavy bag from him. I've just finished his washing.'

The two children went to meet Tolly, and he was very glad to give them his bag of shopping. His dog raced to meet him in delight, barking loudly. His beloved master was back again! Scamper, who was with the children, jumped up eagerly at the old man, too, for he knew him well. Tolly laughed and sat down on an old wooden seat he had made years ago.

'That hill!' he said. 'It gets steeper and steeper, I do declare! I'll get my breath in a minute. So you've made friends with Codger, have you? Fourteen years old, he is, and as good as any five-year-old. Down, Codger, you'll be tearing the young lady's jumper!'

'Oh, I don't mind him jumping at me,' said Janet. 'I think he's a fine little dog. He's got such a nice face too. I like dogs with nice faces. Some have rather fierce ones.'

'Aye, he's a good, kind little dog,' said Tolly. 'When I broke my leg two years since, and laid out there in the rain, at the bottom of the hill, Codger stayed with me all night long. Wet and cold he was, and miserable, but he warmed me all he could, and when morning came, he left me and went to the farmer's place, and pulled at his coat to make him come to me. Aye, he's a good little fellow. My old horse is a good 'un too. I'm a lucky man I am – I've got the two best friends a man can have – a horse and a dog. Come and see the old horse.'

They went to the old, draughty, tumbledown cottage. A brown and white horse put his great head out over a half-door, and nuzzled Tolly and the children. He tried to nuzzle Codger too, but he couldn't reach far enough down over the door. Codger leapt up and licked him on the nose. Tolly undid the door catch and the great horse lumbered

out at once, keeping close to Tolly.

The old man fondled both the dog and the horse, talking to them gently. He looked tired and ill. The little woman in the house came out with a cup of tea for him.

'Here, old man, you come and sit down after that long walk up the hill,' she said. 'You leave your horse be, he's all right. You're for ever a-mothering of him, and bless me if he doesn't mother you too – or try to. Look at him nuzzling about you!

Or maybe you've biscuits in your pockets?'

'Yes, yes, I have – and old Brownie knows it,' said old Tolly.

'You'll have to look after him well!' said the little woman, jokingly. 'There's horse-thieves about this district, so I've heard. One of these nights they'll come and steal your old horse away!'

The old man sat down suddenly on a near-by seat. He looked upset. 'HORSE-thieves!' he said. 'They'd like my Brownie, so they would. He's got good blood in him, Brownie has. The prizes he won when he was younger! I've got them all in the cottage. You must see them, youngsters, you must see them. Horse-thieves you say, Ma'am, horse-thieves! Where can I put my Brownie?'

'If you think there *is* any danger of Brownie being stolen, bring him down to our stable,' said Peter. 'We had already decided it would be a good place for him to live, if you'd like him to. He can't go back to that horrid farmer. And you could bring your little dog Codger too – see how he has made friends with Scamper! Goodness, he can run as fast as our spaniel – faster! Do come down to stay at the farm, and bring the horse and dog. You can have the shepherd's old hut. He's not using it now the lambing season's over.'

'Yes now, Mr Tolly, you do that,' said the little woman, who had been listening all the time. 'You take your horse down to Peter's stables, and Codger as well. If you can have the shepherd's hut, you'll be right grand in it! Go on now – I'll get my sister Agnes to keep an eye on you and the cottage – she'll do your shopping for you too. You go this very minute, with the children. I know their mother, I've worked for her at spring-cleaning time. She'll maybe give you an easy job or two to do. And while you're gone I'll give your old cottage a right good turn-out!'

The old man didn't quite know what to say. Peter took his arm. 'You come with us. You *couldn't* let Brownie be stolen. He'll be safe in our stable. Come along, come along!'

Before old Tolly quite knew what was happening he found himself being led down the hill to the valley below, where the farm lay, peaceful and lovely. Brownie and Codger followed behind. Tolly was quite bemused and certainly more than a little scared by the mention of horse-stealing. His long memory stretched through the years, bringing back vivid pictures of his sorrow when horse-stealers had taken six of his most-prized shire-horses.

'Aye,' he suddenly said, out loud. 'Aye! I reckon

old Brownie would be safe down in your father's stables, youngster – and I'll be sleeping alongside of him. Mebbe your Dad has got a few jobs I can still do. I don't like working for Mr Dinneford now – he's hard, he is, and he don't understand that animals have got to be loved as well as fed. He don't love even a lamb – no, nor even his dog. And he was going to shoot old Brownie that's worked for him for years – just because he hurt his back legs working for him.'

'Don't worry any more,' said Peter and Janet together. But the old fellow went on worrying. 'You see – old Brownie's really Mr Dinneford's, not mine – but I've cared for him all the years, and he's like a brother to me now. It nigh broke my heart when that heavy-loaded cart ran on to his poor old back legs!'

Janet was upset to see a large tear run slowly down old Tolly's rough cheek. She slipped her arm through his. 'Don't you worry any more,' she said. 'You shall come and live in our shepherd's old hut, and when Brownie is in our stable, quite safe, you'll feel happy.'

'The vet can come and see his legs and make sure that they get quite better,' said Peter, saying every-thing that he could possibly think of, to comfort the old fellow. But this didn't bring any comfort at all! Tolly stopped as if he had been shot, and pulled his arm away from Peter. He faced him, looking very scared.

'The vet – Mr Whistler?' he said. 'I'll have to go to prison if his bill isn't paid. That's what Farmer Dinneford told me! Go to prison, and leave my dog and Brownie behind! Mr Dinneford wouldn't bother to feed them – they'd be dead when I came out. No, no, young sir, you be very kind, I know, but I can't have that Mr Whistler any more. Mr

Dinneford, he says I'm to pay those bills, because he reckons it was my fault that old Brownie got so badly hurt. He knows I think of Brownie as my own – I've looked after him so many years now, and we've worked together for the master, and . . .'

He broke off and bent down to pat Codger, who was very worried because his master sounded so angry and so sad. He licked old Tolly's hand gently.

'How much money would Farmer Dinneford ask for Brownie?' said Peter.

'Old Brownie wouldn't fetch much now, young sir,' said Tolly. 'He's old, and now that his back legs are weak-like, because of that heavy cart running into them, he's not all that good for farm-work. But he still costs as much in fodder, and those vet-bills are a real worry. I'm right down afraid that Mr Dinneford will think he's not worth his keep any more, and – and will have him shot.'

'Don't you worry,' said Peter, feeling quite desperate. 'We'll see that he's not shot. Er – Janet and I are thinking of buying him ourselves – and then he'd be quite safe, wouldn't he?'

Janet stared at Peter in the greatest surprise. *Buy old Brownie?* Where would they get the money from? What would their father say? Would Farmer Dinneford sell him? Yes, probably – but he would put a good price on the old horse if he thought that somebody else wanted him! She tugged at Peter's arm.

But he shook off her hand impatiently. 'Well, Tolly, what price do you think Farmer Dinneford would want?'

Tolly had been so surprised when he heard Peter say that he and Janet were thinking of buying Brownie that he just couldn't say a word. He gaped at Peter, opening and shutting his mouth like a fish.

'Well – what price *would* Brownie be?' asked Peter again. 'Fifty pounds, do you think?'

'Oh more than that, youngster, more than that,' said Tolly, finding his voice. 'Why, you and the little Missy couldn't possibly buy a horse. What pocket-money do you get – one pound a week?'

'We've saved up quite a bit,' said Peter. 'But we couldn't pay more than fifty pounds between us.'

Tolly shook his head. 'Mr Dinneford would say one hundred pounds, mebbe more,' he said. 'Though I'd say meself that's too high a price for an old horse that's got poor hind legs. Them legs might go weak any day, and then Brownie would be no good at anything except cropping the grass.'

Peter gave a heavy sigh. What a pity he wasn't grown up. He could then do as his father did – go to

the bank and take out quite large sums of money. He could buy Brownie easily then!

'Er – my friends and I are going to help to pay the vet's bill – Mr Whistler's account,' said Peter. 'I thought I'd tell you now, to save you worrying. We haven't got the money yet, but we're earning some. One of my friends is working for the vet at night – taking round medicines. He reckons he'll earn ten pounds fifty pence in two weeks.'

'And Dad says that if we muck out the stable and keep it decent when Brownie comes, he'll provide the old horse with free fodder,' said Janet. 'And I bet the others are thinking of some more ideas too. So don't you worry, Mr Tolly. We'll be sure to get enough money for the vet – and Brownie will be safe from harm down in our stable – he'll be happy with the other horses. They're nice ones – they don't kick or anything like that. I'm sure they'd love Brownie.'

'Oh Missy, what's all this you're saying?' said old Tolly, staring at the two children in surprise. 'I've heard your Dad is a good kind man, and it's certain that he's got children like himself! All right, Brownie and me, we'll leave Mr Dinneford. I'll leave Brownie with you, and come to sleep in the stables at night – and work out a week's notice with Mr Dinneford. He'd be after me if I left at a moment's notice. And don't you say a word to anyone about my Brownie being with you – in case the farmer hears of it and comes after him. Not a word!'

'We certainly won't!' said Janet. 'Look, here we are. Let's go into the stable. We've already chosen a stall for Brownie, next to a nice kind horse – and there's plenty of good fresh hay for him!'

They all went into the stables, Codger wagging his tail fast. This was quite an adventure! Brownie gave a little whinny, as he smelt the horsy-smell, and tapped on the floor with his foot as if to say, 'Very nice. Very nice indeed!'

There were no other horses in the stables. They were all out working, or feeding in the fields. Brownie began to nibble at the fodder in his stall.

'Look at that now. He's at home already,' said Peter. 'Good old horse. You're safe here, Brownie. Come down tonight and sleep in the stables with him, Mr Tolly. You'll *both* be safe – and happy – and warm. You come down here, see?'

Five

The police vet calls

AFTER tea time that same day Tolly arrived at the farm to sleep in the stables with Brownie. He found the children's father waiting to see him.

'Ah, Tolly – I see you've put your horse – or it is Mr Dinneford's horse? – safely in our stable,' he said. 'Well, I'm glad to see it there, as, according to the children, there's a chance of it being shot because of the accident it had. But – er – what does Mr Dinneford, your master, say about this arrangement? I hope you told him. I've examined the horse's hind legs myself, and they're not right yet, by any means. I doubt if he'll be any good for farmwork now. Nice horse too – good strong animal.'

'Yes, sir,' said Tolly, anxiously. 'The vet said his legs *would* get better, he thought – but slowly, sir. And I expect you know that Mr Dinneford, he's impatient-like, and he won't keep any animal that can't do much, but eats its head off all the time, and costs money in fodder, and . . .'

'Yes, yes. I know your master's reputation,' said Peter's father. 'Well, I'm willing to let you and the horse sleep in my stable at night, in order that Brownie shan't be shot. If you've given notice to your master, I'll take you on myself, as I'm short of a man. You'd do general work – horses – sheep – field-work, and so on. What about it?'

'Well, sir, I'm very, very grateful indeed. I've given in my notice, sir, and Mr Dinneford, he was downright angry with me, and said I must go at once. And, sir, he said he was going to shoot Brownie tonight, as I wouldn't be there to see to him and his bad legs. They have to be rubbed at night, sir, with this liniment stuff that the vet gave me. The master, he said the vet was making a fuss, but this stuff is good, sir. It's helping Brownie's legs, I know it is.'

'Right. Keep it then, because you'll be in charge of Brownie, with the two children as your helpers,' said Peter's father. 'And don't worry about the horse – he'll be safe here. In any case I shall get in touch with the police in case of any trouble.'

'Yes, sir,' said Tolly and touched his cap. Well! he thought, this is the kind of man I want to work for. Knows his own mind – kind – sensible – forthright. And I've got old Brownie too. What'll happen if Mr Dinneford comes after him, though?

But Peter's father had thought about that. He had telephoned the police and had told them about his engagement of Tolly, and the fact that the man had brought the horse to him.

'Dinneford was going to shoot it – or so he says,' said Peter's father to the police sergeant who answered the telephone. 'I'm willing to buy it off him at a reasonable price to save its being shot. The horse's hind legs are no good at the moment, so he's a bit of an old crock – but they may mend. Shall I get the vet in to say what he's worth at the moment – in case Dinneford makes a fuss, and puts an enormous price on the horse?'

'No, sir – don't get Mr Whistler,' said the police sergeant. 'Better get our own police vet – he'll be here soon to look over the police horses we have for our two mounted police – the ones that go round the markets when there are great crowds about. Wonderful what a horse can do, when crowds gather, and won't clear away. People scatter like sheep when the police horses gallop up! I'll ask our vet to go down to your place tonight, sir. Thank you. Good evening, sir!'

So that night the police vet came along, smart and

spruce, and very quick. He examined old Brownie from head to tail, from shoulders to hooves, looked into his mouth and even inside his ears! Tolly stood near by, looking very anxious. He didn't know *what* to think!

If he says the horse is fine, strong as can be, healthy and able to work hard, it'll mean he's worth a lot of money, and I shan't be able to pay the price for him, he thought. And if they think he's a poor old horse, because of his accident, I'll not dare to work him, in case of harming him. I don't know WHAT to wish for!

The police vet went to talk to Peter's father when he had finished.

'Well, sir,' he said, 'he's a good horse, as good as ever he was. But he does need gentle handling, sir. He's a bit nervy. That may be because of the accident he had, of course. If he could be handled now by someone he knows and trusts, he'll soon be all right – but don't let any stranger handle him, sir – he'll get more nervy, and not be a bit of use to anyone in a few months' time. Gently does it, sir, with that horse. I'd take him off your hands myself, if I could. He's a beauty!'

'Thanks very much indeed, Sergeant,' said Peter's father, pleased. 'You've said more or less what I myself thought. What would he be worth now, if anyone bought him?'

'Well, sir, not much if you sell him to a stranger, or to a bad handler,' said the vet. 'He seems happy enough here. Why don't you keep him? You wouldn't get more than fifty or seventy-five pounds for him now, with those damaged back legs. But a patient owner, who wouldn't work the horse at all for say, six months, would find he had a first-class horse at the end of that time, strong, willing, and as good as ever!'

'Fine, fine!' said Peter's father, and the two children, who were listening, squeezed each other's arms in delight. Now Brownie would be bought – and kept. And Tolly would come to them, and have a good job, and be with the horse he loved!

How they hoped that Mr Dinneford wouldn't want Brownie any more! Anyway, he'd be safe with them for some time, recovering slowly in their stables!

Six

Brownie gets a new home

WHEN the police vet had gone, Peter's father and mother, Mr Tolly and the two children and Scamper went into the summer-house for a good long talk.

'We have to decide straight away what we can do about Brownie,' said Mr Tolly, anxiously. 'He can't go back to Mr Dinneford, sir, to the farm. He'd be worked and worked there, or shot, maybe, and he's not as strong as he was. Have you examined his hind legs, sir? What did *you* think of them?'

'Well, it's a toss-up, Tolly,' said Peter's father. 'With careful, friendly handling Brownie might be as good as ever in six months' time – but his hind legs are definitely not strong enough for hard work yet. But who's going to keep a horse for six months or maybe longer and not work him – and possibly find at the end of that time he's no good at all? It would be money down the drain for anyone who bought him then.'

'Sir – would you tell Mr Dinneford that?' asked

Tolly, anxiously. 'If he'd sell Brownie now, while he would go cheap, I'd buy him. I wouldn't work him at all for six months, and I'd be glad to buy his fodder and see to him. I shall soon be leaving the farm up on the hill there – I can't work for Mr Dinneford any longer, and anyway, I've given in my notice. I could go somewhere with Brownie, and get a job for myself, and see that the old horse was quiet and happy till his legs were quite mended.'

'You know you can stay here, Tolly,' said Peter's father. 'You're an old man now, you want a quiet job, with not too much heavy work. If you like to come to me and see to my horses for me, as I said, you'd be welcome. Sleep in the stables, or in the shepherd's old hut, or out on the hills, wherever you please.'

'Thank you kindly, sir, you're a real gentleman,' said Tolly, warmly. He turned to Peter. 'Yes – you're lucky, you are – that's a *real* gentleman your father is, and just see that you grow up like him, young man. You won't go far wrong, then!'

Peter grinned, delighted at this praise of his father. 'Are you going to buy Brownie from my father?' he said. 'That's if Mr Dinneford will sell him, of course – and I bet he will if he thinks he can't work Brownie for ages.'

'Young man, I haven't even five pounds to my name!' said Tolly. 'Else I'd buy him this very minute. What with having to pay out for my rent and fire and light and clothes and food, and with having to help an old invalid sister of mine, I don't have as much money to spare as you have! But I'm going to ask your Dad if he'll keep back so much of my wages each week, so that when I've about fifty pounds saved, I can buy Brownie for my very own. That's if Mr Dinneford will sell the horse to your father, of course!'

'Mr Tolly, would you let us share Brownie with you, if we pay *half* the fifty pounds for him?' asked Janet. 'If he's coming to live here with us, I'd so like to think we could share him.'

'You can share him all you like, when he's mine,' said Tolly. 'You can consider him half yours and half mine. He'd like that. He likes children. You don't need to pay me.'

'Oh but we must,' said Peter. 'We shouldn't feel as if he really *was* half ours, if we hadn't paid something for him. We'll buy the half with the bad legs, if you like, so that you can have the best half.'

'Well, whatever will you say next?' said Tolly, astonished. 'Now look – you save up and buy half of him if you badly want to. I know how you feel. I feel like that myself. I shan't be happy till I've paid over that fifty pounds to your father and then can look at old Brownie and say to myself, "You beauty, you're mine. I've worked for you, and cared for you, and paid for you – and now you're mine to look after for the rest of *your* life!" There's something about horses that just *gets* me. And old Brownie – well, he's – he's . . .'

'The best horse in the world!' finished Peter, with a laugh. 'I feel rather like that about Scamper, our dog. You know – best dog in all the world! Are you, Scamper? Cook says you're just a scrounger with muddy feet and an inquisitive nose. But *I* think you're the Best Dog in the World!'

'Woof!' said Scamper, wagging his tail very fast indeed. 'WOOF!' He ran to Peter and licked first one of his hands and then the other. Peter patted him lovingly. 'Old fuss-pot! You do love a bit of petting, don't you? Good lad Scamper! Good dog, then!'

Peter's father was standing by, very much amused by all this. 'Well – when we've all finished saying nice things to each other, I think we'd better go in,' he said. 'It will soon be supper-time. Hello – who's this?'

There was a clattering of hooves, and a pony-cart

drew up outside the front gate. 'WHOA!' said an enormous voice.

'It's Mr Dinneford!' said Janet, in a fright. 'Oh Daddy, Daddy – DON'T let him take Brownie away, will you?'

'Of course not. Go indoors,' said her father. 'Both of you. Look out of the window if you like, but no listening. You stay here, Tolly.'

The children fled indoors and pulled a curtain so that they might look out and see what happened. Oh dear – how dreadful if Brownie was taken away!

They could hear loud voices, but couldn't understand a word. The three men were very angry.

'Tolly! What do you mean by stealing my horse?' shouted Mr Dinneford.

'You said you were going to shoot him, so he was as good as dead, wasn't he?' shouted back Tolly. 'I'm not going to let a good horse like that be shot, even if he *has* got useless hind legs.'

'Useless! You're about right there!' yelled Mr Dinneford. 'Why should I keep a useless horse, eating his head off in my stables? He's *my* horse, isn't he? Can't I do what I like with my own horses?'

'Within reason, Dinneford, within reason,' said Peter's father. 'But *you* need horses that are strong enough to pull very heavy loads – and that horse will

never pull loads again. He will be quite useless to you. Why don't you sell him for what you can get?'

'How do you know he's useless?' yelled Mr Dinneford, angrier than ever.

'Well – we had the police vet here just a little while ago,' said Mr Tolly. 'And I'm afraid he didn't give a very good report.'

'What did he say?' asked Mr Dinneford, rather taken aback to hear that the police vet had been along. He wondered if Mr Tolly had told the police that he, Mr Dinneford, had proposed to shoot the horse.

'He said that the horse was nervy, sir, because of his accident,' said Mr Tolly, 'and wouldn't be a bit of use to anyone for some time. He said you wouldn't get more than seventy-five pounds for him now.'

'Seventy-five pounds! And I paid one hundred and fifty!' shouted the exasperated Mr Dinneford. 'And who'd give me seventy-five pounds for him like he is now, tell me that!'

'Well – maybe he'll be better in a few months' time,' said Mr Tolly, 'and then . . .'

'Oh, don't tell me fairy stories about that horse! Those hind legs will *never* get better – they'll get worse! I shan't even be able to get fifty pounds for him, let alone seventy-five, you know that!'

'I'll give you fifty,' said Mr Tolly, unexpectedly. 'And that's because I'm fond of him and don't want to see him shot.'

'Well, you're a nincompoop if you think that horse is worth even *fifty* pounds!' raged Mr Dinneford. 'I don't believe the police said the horse was worth a penny! He should be shot!'

'Right. If you don't want to sell him, take him away and go,' said Peter's father, in a stern, voice.

Mr Dinneford swung round. 'Do *you* want to give me fifty pounds for him?' he said. 'Are you an idiot too, like Tolly here?'

'I may be,' said Peter's father, 'but it's worth fifty pounds to be rid of you. Either go and take the horse with you – or leave it here and take this fifty pounds. But make up your mind!'

'All right. I'll take the money,' said Mr Dinneford, a little ashamed of himself as he saw Peter's father's disgusted face. 'Good riddance to a nuisance of a horse, I say. Thanks for the money, sir. Good evening.'

He pocketed the money and away he went striding off, leaving the horse behind. It had been scared of the angry voices, and had gone to Tolly for comfort. 'Now, now!' he said, stroking the soft nose. 'He's gone. You won't hear his loud voice again. You don't belong to him any more.' And he led the horse to Peter's father.

'Well, Tolly – the horse is *yours*,' said Peter's father. 'That is – if you want him. I'll deduct five pounds a week from your wages till the money is paid off. That be all right?'

'Yes, sir. Thank you very much, sir,' said Tolly,

his face one big smile. He put his arm round the horse's neck. 'Well, my beauty! You belong to *me* now – or you will in a few weeks' time – say five weeks. Could you, sir, deduct *ten* pounds a week from my wages for five weeks? That will clear the debt. Ha – fifty pounds of very, very good horse! You wait till a few months have gone by, my beauty, and you'll be as good as ever you were! You'll be worth your weight in gold!'

'Very well, Tolly,' said Peter's father, smiling at the old man's joy. 'You'll be less ten pounds a week till the debt is paid off – and then Brownie will be yours for keeps. And a fine horse he is too, except for those weak back legs. But they'll improve. He'll be a fine horse again before very long – and you deserve to have him, Tolly. Take him off now and bed him down in the stables. He'll be happy to have you fussing round him again, I've no doubt!'

Seven

Tolly and Brownie

As soon as the children saw that Mr Dinneford had gone off and that Tolly was leading the horse to the stables, they raced out of the house to him.

'Tolly! What happened? Is he yours? You said you hadn't enough money to buy him. Oh, isn't he a darling?'

Brownie nuzzled both children gently. He liked them very much.

'He's mine all right,' said Tolly, proudly, as he backed the horse into his new quarters. 'There you are, my beauty. You stay there awhile till we find some supper for you and some water. Ha – someone's put plenty of good straw bedding down for you. You'll be well-off here, old horse.'

'Have you really bought him, Tolly? Was Mr Dinneford very angry? We heard him shouting,' said Janet.

'Yes. I've bought him – though he won't be rightly mine for five weeks,' said Tolly, rubbing the horse's long nose lovingly. 'Your Dad's going to take ten pounds a week off my wages till Brownie's paid for – fifty pounds your father gave for him – but *I* wouldn't sell him if you offered me five thousand!'

'Don't forget that you promised us we could have half of him for our own,' said Janet. 'We shall give you our share of the price as soon as we can. We've got some money in our money-boxes, and Granny is coming next week – she always gives us about two pounds each.'

'Now don't you worry about the money,' said Tolly. 'You don't *need* to pay me a penny for your share of him. I'll willingly share him with you. It isn't often children love horses like you two. You deserve half of my Brownie!'

Brownie was very pleased with his new stable. He threw back his head and sent a loud, delighted whinny through the whole place. The two other horses who were there were startled, and said 'hrrrrumphs' in surprise.

'He'll be pleased when he goes out into the fields,' said Peter. 'I bet he'll gallop all over the place, and make friends with any animal there, horse, sheep, or dog!'

'Your Dad's been a right good sort over Brownie and Codger,' said Tolly. 'Well, I must go back to Mr

Dinneford's and get all my things. Stay quiet now, Brownie. I'll be back to sleep with you tonight. Can't have anyone stealing you!'

He said goodbye to the children and went back up the hill to Mr Dinneford's farm. Now – if that Mr Dinneford started on at him about old Brownie, he'd tell him a few truths and see what he made of those!

But Mr Dinneford didn't come near Tolly. He was now wishing that he hadn't told him to go! Tolly was a fine, trustworthy worker. Whatever would he do without him?

I'll clear up everything, and leave it all shipshape! thought Tolly. I'll miss all the horses – but there, my new master will have plenty of them for me to care for!

That night Tolly went to see that Brownie was safe and happy in his new stable. In the afternoon the old horse had been out in the fields, getting to know one or two of the other horses who were grazing there. Then he had brought beets to the yard in a cart – a very light cart indeed, which did not strain his back legs at all.

Tolly watched him, very pleased. 'Those back legs of yours are better even than last week!' he told Brownie. 'Now you be careful of them, see – and lie

down in your stable as much as you can. Don't stand all the time – even if you *do* want to talk to the horses next to you!'

Brownie had given a happy little whinny, as if he had understood every word. He sensed that his master was happy, for some reason, and so he was happy too. He wondered why he was in such a strange place, but as long as he could hear Tolly whistling somewhere not too far off, he was content.

And now here was Tolly settling down on an old mattress in the empty stall next to Brownie. The old horse was delighted. He couldn't *see* Tolly there, but he could smell his familiar smell, and he was comforted to feel that Tolly was nearby, as he stood in his stall in the strange stable.

'Now I'm here, near you, old horse,' said Tolly in a low voice. 'Sleep well. Lie down in your straw. I'm here, close to you. Nice and warm, isn't it? Good night, Brownie. You don't need to be afraid of horse-thieves while *I'm* close beside you! And old Codger is here too, in the straw. Say good night, Codger!' And Codger gave a small bark as if to say 'Good night! Sleep well!'

Codger was the first one out and about the next morning. He scrabbled out of the straw in the stall

he had slept in, and went to lick his master's face.

'Don't,' said Tolly, sleepily. 'How many times have I told . . .' And off he went to sleep again before he could finish his sentence!

Codger looked up at the half-door that shut him and his master into the stall. Yes – he could just about jump it. He crouched – leapt as high as he could – and just failed to get over the half-door. Instead he fell back heavily on to Tolly who awoke with a jump and a shout.

'HEY! WHO'S THIS? THIEVES, THIEVES!'

'Wuff!' said Codger, in a small, scared voice. Oh dear – what had he done? Awakened his master, and made him think there were thieves about!

'You silly little idiot, Codger!' said Tolly, crossly. 'What did you jump on me for? It isn't time to get up. Now you've woken up the horses. Hark at them hrrrumphing! I'll have to get out of this stall and quieten them!'

So up he got and went from stall to stall, patting and stroking, trying to quieten the frightened horses. 'Anyone would think horse-thieves were about!' he grumbled, as the horses stamped and shuffled uneasily. 'Now just you lie quiet, Codger, and don't move so much as a whisker. I want to go to sleep!'

Eight

Next morning

WHEN Peter and Janet woke up the next morning they each remembered about Tolly, and how he had bought old Brownie. Janet lay and thought about it for a little while, and then she slipped out of her room, and ran to wake Peter.

He was so sound asleep that it was hard to wake him. She shook him and pummelled him, but he just gave little grunts and turned away.

'Peter! You *know* you're not as deeply asleep as all that!' said Janet, crossly. 'All right. I've a pin here and I'll just see if *that* will wake you.'

Peter sat up immediately! He was cross and frowning. 'What's the matter? Don't you dare to stick that pin into me, you horrible girl. It must be awfully early in the morning. What's the matter?'

'It *isn't* early. It's only ten minutes to breakfast time,' said Janet. 'Do get up. I want to be down early to breakfast, and to talk to you about calling a meeting of the Secret Seven. We MUST let the others know about Tolly and Brownie and Codger. We've done everything on our own so far, and we oughtn't to do any more without at least *tell*ing them!'

'All right. Call a meeting then. I'm going to sleep again,' said Peter, snuggling down under the bed-clothes once more.

'You really are a stupid, silly sleepyhead!' said Janet, crossly. She got off the bed. 'All right, I'll take you at your word. Go to sleep all the morning if you want to. *I'm* going to call a Secret Seven meeting myself, see. I'll go round IMMEDIATELY after breakfast and warn everyone. I'll tell them you're not feeling too good, and that I'll take the meeting, and be its head, instead of you.'

'You will NOT!' said Peter, fiercely. He flung off the bed-clothes so violently that they fell all over Janet and she was nearly smothered. 'Go away, you horrid girl. I'll turn you out of the Secret Seven if you go on like this!'

Janet gave a chuckle and went off to her own room. Ah now – *now* they would be sure to have a Secret Seven meeting. How she loved them! There was quite a lot to report too. 'I'll take some of the chocolates that Auntie gave me last time she was here. And I'll ask Mrs Simmons for some of the ginger cake she made two days ago. It was an enormous one – there must surely be lots left! There's such heaps to talk about we'll *need* something to eat. We'll talk about Tolly – and Brownie – and how Daddy bought Brownie for fifty pounds, and that half Brownie is ours – and Tolly is sleeping in the stable with Brownie and our other horses . . .'

There was still quite a while before breakfast and Janet scribbled as many Secret Seven notices as she could.

'IMPORTANT: *A Secret Seven Meeting will be held in our shed at ten o'clock sharp, to report further proceedings on the complaint that Bob Smith made at our last meeting. Please come, as plenty has happened. Bring sweets or chocolates or ginger beer if possible.*

Janet. Secret Seven Club.'

Peter was cross with her at breakfast, so she didn't say a word about the meeting. Soon Peter spoke to her commandingly. 'After breakfast we'll go and write those notes to the others. Buck up. There's not much time if we want to hold it at ten.'

'My *dear* boy – *I* wrote all the notes while you were half-awake!' said Janet. 'I was afraid you might not wake up even for breakfast!'

'Don't be an idiot,' said Peter. 'How *dare* you write notes to the Secret Seven members without even asking *me* what you're to put.'

'Well – it wasn't much *good* asking you,' said Janet. 'You were so sound asleep. I just hadn't the heart to wake you properly, you looked so very peaceful. Still – I can tear the notes up if you like. Perhaps you *had* better write them, and dictate every single one to yourself.'

'No – no, don't tear them up!' said Peter, as Janet took up the little pile of notes. He was alarmed at such an idea. *He* didn't want to have to begin writing out the whole lot again himself!

'Well – will you take them round to the others then?' said Janet. 'I'll get the shed ready.'

'All right. I'll go immediately,' said Peter. 'I *would* like to go and see how Tolly and Brownie and Codger are first, though. I dreamed about Brownie all night!'

'What did you dream?' asked Janet, with interest. Peter sometimes had very, very interesting and exciting dreams.

'I dreamt he ran away with Codger because thieves came,' said Peter. 'And please don't remind me of it because I shall be scared of it coming true.'

'Baby!' said Janet. 'Buck up with your breakfast. I'll go and make the beds.'

Peter gobbled the rest of his breakfast, snatched up the notes Janet had written and tore off to deliver them. He saw nobody at all as he pushed them through each letter-box and rang the bell before trotting off again down the front path. He was home in record time, and went to find old Tolly. Janet rushed after him.

Tolly was helping to milk the cows, and looked very happy. The other men had made him welcome, and had admired Brownie so much that Tolly nearly burst with pride.

'How's Brownie?' asked Janet, smiling as the old man placed a bucket under another cow, to milk it.

'Brownie's fine!' said Tolly, as the good rich milk squirted into the pail. 'Fine! He likes being with so many other horses. He's perked up a lot, Miss Janet. You go and say good morning to him. He'll be pleased to see you. He'll be giving you gallops on his back over the fields and hills before you know where you are!'

Janet went to see the old horse. His head was over the stall-door, and she opened it and slipped in beside him.

'Brownie! Did you have a good night? Are you

happy here? You weren't frightened, were you, the
first night in a strange place?'

'Hrrrrrumph!' said Brownie, and pushed the girl
gently with his nose. She rubbed her hand up and
down it.

'I like you, Brownie. I like you. Your legs will soon be QUITE all right, won't they? I'm sure they will!'

The other horses now had their noses over *their* doors, waiting for Janet to come by. They all knew her, of course, and loved her. She was always gentle and loving to them.

A bell rang out from somewhere. 'That's the bell to say I'm wanted indoors!' she told the horse. 'I must fly. Did Tolly sleep with you last night? I've just been to say good morning to him.'

And away she went, her hair flying in the wind just like a horse's mane!

Nine

Another meeting

THE two children soon gathered up the things they wanted to take to the meeting-shed. Mrs Simmons had been very nice and had given them half the gingerbread cake. 'It wants eating up,' she said. 'It's getting a wee bit stale, but you won't mind that, *I* know. And here's an apple for each one of you. Gardener brought them in – he says they're only windfalls, but they'll be sweet.'

'Oh, thank you!' said Janet, pleased. 'I usually buy some sweets or something for the meetings, but I haven't enough time now – not till I find my purse anyway – and goodness knows where that's gone! Buck up, Peter. I'm just going down to the shed. The others will be here in half a tick.'

'I'm just going to make a few notes,' said Peter. 'I think we ought to find out if anyone has got money in to help to pay the vet's bill. We ought to begin to pay some of it off. We promised we would.'

'Well, I've got fifty pence,' said Janet. 'I didn't

earn it, though. I found it on our gravel path this morning. I only hope I can remember where I put it!'

'Lucky thing!' said Peter. 'I'm taking a collection this morning at the meeting, so you *could* put it in that. Every little helps.'

'I was going to, of course,' said Janet. 'And I've opened my money-box too. Mother said I could take half of what I had there, to help to pay the vet's fees, if I really wanted to. I said that I'd do anything to help poor old Tolly.'

'So would I,' said Peter. 'I'll get *my* money-box too. I wish I hadn't spent so much on bull's-eyes lately. But I've had several good books to read – and a bull's-eye is just right for a good book. It lasts and lasts!'

At five minutes to ten they were down at the shed. Clean writing-paper was there, a pencil and a pen and a rubber. Even a ruler, though Janet felt sure that Peter wouldn't want *that*! Their money-boxes were there too, each with their keys in them for unlocking.

'Gingerbread cake!' said Janet, putting a plate on the table. 'A bit stale, but what does that matter? And an apple each. These two are a bit bad, Peter, *we'd* better have those and give the good ones to the others.'

Another meeting

'Right,' said Peter. 'Oh, you've brought some of your chocs too. Good! Shut the door, quick. I can hear someone coming. It might be Susie, that tiresome sister of Jack's and we're not having her in!'

Knock-knock.

'Password!' shouted Peter and Janet together. A plaintive voice came from outside. 'Peter – Janet – is it *still* "Scamper" because if there's a new password, I've forgotten it.'

'Enter!' called Peter, and in came Pam, with Barbara close behind her. 'Hello!' said Pam, 'I *thought* we hadn't changed the password. Hello, Scamper! How do you like being a password?'

Scamper licked her bare legs, and sat down by Janet. He liked these meetings. There were always titbits of some sort!

One by one the others came, and soon the meeting was complete. Bob was there too, looking very thrilled. 'Any news of old Mr Tolly?' asked Colin. 'I don't seem to have seen *any* of you at all. I've had to do a lot of swotting.'

'Now,' said Peter, 'I will declare the meeting open, and ask the members if they have anything to say. You will remember what we talked about at the last meeting, and how we were all going to try and help Mr Tolly in some way.'

'Let's tell *them* what's happened since the last meeting,' interrupted Janet.

'Yes, yes – do tell us,' said Pam, Jack, and George all together, while Colin, Barbara, and Bob nodded their heads. 'We're just bursting to know!'

'Well actually, quite a *lot* has happened,' said Peter. 'Old Mr Tolly brought his horse Brownie here to us yesterday, and it's in our stable now. That horrid Mr Dinneford was very, very angry with Tolly. He said that Tolly had ruined the horse's back legs, and . . .'

'Oh – is the horse *here*?' said Pam, in excitement, and Peter frowned.

'Don't interrupt when I'm speaking,' he said. 'I'm the head of the Secret Seven, aren't I?'

'Ooooh, sorry, Peter,' said Pam, going very red. 'It's just that I so badly wanted . . .'

'Be quiet! Sh!' said everyone, and Pam sank back into her chair, half sulky.

'Where was I now?' said Peter. 'Oh yes – when the police vet came, he said that the horse's legs were quite badly damaged and that he was in a very nervy state – but that with gentle handling and kindness, he might be quite all right again in a few months' time. He said his legs were to be rubbed with some kind of stuff – Janet knows more about that than I do – she's done a little of the rubbing because she has gentle hands. And that's about all.'

'Oh *no*, Peter – you've forgotten the most important part – about *buying* the horse!' said Janet. 'That's what we want the *money* for!'

'Why – do you want the horse to belong to *every*body in the Secret Seven Club, instead of just us and Tolly?' said Peter. 'That's silly.'

'No, it isn't silly!' said Barbara, who was fond of horses. 'I'd just LOVE to think I owned part of a horse. I once owned half a dog. I and my cousin, who lived next door, shared it between us – we each put down half the money. I really do think that the dog *liked* being shared. I'm sure Brownie would. Think of having *seven* people spoiling him instead of just one. What a wonderful time he'd have! Fancy the Secret Seven owning half a horse! I bet no other club in the world does that!'

'Where *is* this horse?' asked Colin. 'I didn't see him when I came past the stables. They seemed empty to me!'

'Somebody must have stolen him then!' cried Janet, jumping up. 'Or left the door open. Peter, did you?'

'No! I haven't been *near* the stables!' said Peter, jumping up too. 'Oh – Oh, I say – just look!'

And, as they all turned towards the open window of the shed, they saw a very, very pleasant sight. Brownie was putting his long nose inside! He had somehow got out of his stall, and had heard the sound of voices, and come to investigate! What a lovely thing he looked, staring shyly in at the window. 'Hhrumph!' he said, in a mild, inquiring voice.

'He wants a piece of gingerbread!' said Pam, and would have given him the whole lot if Peter hadn't snatched the plate from her!

'The meeting is put off for half an hour,' said Peter, desperately. 'We really *can't* have Brownie at a meeting. STOP barking, Scamper. Oh goodness – there they go together, tearing over the lawn. *Look* at those hoofmarks! Now we're in for trouble!'

It took some time to capture the excited Brownie. *He* thought that it was a wonderful game of 'Dodge About' and 'Don't be Caught' and he darted here and there, over flower beds and vegetable beds and lawns to his heart's content. The gardener and Tolly caught him at last, and led him firmly back to his stable.

'I'm ashamed of you, Brownie!' said the panting Tolly. 'Right – Down – Ashamed – Of You! I'll be working all day long on the beds you've trampled!'

'We'll help!' said the children, and they did. Tolly was very thankful to see the garden more or less itself again before Peter's father came out!

'We were in the middle of a Secret Seven meeting,' said Peter to Tolly. 'I suppose you couldn't come to it now, could you? – we're going to hold the rest of it immediately – in the shed – and we'd like you to tell us a few things.'

'Right,' said Tolly. 'I've got about a quarter of an hour to spare. What meeting is this?'

'We were going to discuss money,' said Peter, leading everyone back into the shed. 'You see, we have promised to pay the vet's fees for Brownie – and we've got some money towards them this morning – and we also want to discuss the *buying* of Brownie.'

They were now all sitting round the shed, looking eagerly at the surprised Tolly. He gazed at the various money-boxes on the table, and at one or two envelopes and purses.

'That's what we've got already towards the vet's fees,' said Pam. 'That's my purse. I weeded my Granny's garden for a day and a half, and she gave me two pounds fifty pence! So *that's* to go towards the vet's fees.'

'And I took care of our neighbour's dog for two

whole days while he was away,' said Jack. 'Awfully nice dog too, it was. *I* didn't take it walks. It took *me* walks! And guess what old Mr Kay gave me for that. He gave me a pound at first – and then when he heard what I was going to do with it – help with the vet's fees, of course – he trebled the money and gave me three pounds!'

'Good *gracious*!' said everyone.

'I'm afraid I wasn't so lucky,' said Colin. '*I* took *two* dogs for walks, but one jumped into a very dirty part of the river, and it came out absolutely *covered* with mud. So I'm afraid I only got seventy-five pence – *and* I had to give the dog a bath too!'

'Bad luck,' said Peter. 'What about you, Barbara?'

'I brought my money-box. I think it has about three pounds fifty pence in it,' said Barbara. 'I had to buy rather a lot of birthday presents – three lots in three weeks – and the last one was two days ago. I'm sure there's only three pounds fifty pence in it now.'

'Bad luck. Never mind, you can always save up a bit more later on', said Peter. 'We shan't be able to pay much of the vet's bill *this* time. George, what about you?'

'Ha!' said George. 'I've got some NEWS. Some weeks ago I went in for a competition for an essay about clubs – the first prize was fifty pounds and . . .'

'You surely didn't win THAT!' shouted Peter, standing up in excitement.

'No, no, I didn't win the first prize of fifty pounds – but I *did* win the second prize – and that was *twenty-five pounds!*' said George, his face glowing. 'I heard this morning. I haven't got the money yet, but Dad says it will come all right. He gave me the twenty-five pounds in advance, so that I could give the whole of it to the vet for his fees for Brownie. I shall give the money back to Dad when my prize money arrives.'

There was a silence. *What* a wonderful thing to do! *What* a gift! Good old George! Now he was being hugged by Janet, and patted on the back by the others!

'Did your parents *say* you could give it towards the vet's fees?' asked Peter.

'Yes. I told them, of course. They were frightfully pleased,' said George. 'In fact, Dad nearly gave me *another* twenty-five pounds to match this one. Mother just stopped him in time!'

The gifts from the others didn't seem very exciting, after hearing about George's magnificent prize of twenty-five pounds! Peter put in his money-box

savings, which amounted to three pounds and seventy-five pence and Janet put in hers which came to two pounds altogether. Bob shyly put in two pounds and twenty-five pence. 'Mostly for errands,' he said.

'How much does it all amount to?' asked Pam, eagerly. 'It looks an awful lot of money now it's out on the table. Enough to pay a dozen vets!'

Peter solemnly and slowly counted the collection of money on the table, including, of course, the exciting, crisp five and twenty pound notes!

'We have here the large sum of forty-four pounds,' he said. 'There!'

Jack lost control of himself in his excitement, and jumped up, cheering so loudly that Scamper fled out of the shed with his tail well down!

'HIP HURRAY! HIP, HIP HIP, HURRAY!' And, of course, everyone joined in, including Tolly, who was almost as excited as the children.

'We've got enough for the vet's fees!' cried Peter, in delight. 'Oh, George – you *are* a brick to put in that twenty-five pounds! We'll never, never, forget that. NEVER! What a happy ending to a WONDERFUL meeting! HURRAY!'

Ten

Off to see the vet

TOLLY hadn't said a single word. He had sat open-mouthed, listening to the excited children in the greatest wonder. He kept staring at the twenty pound note on the table as if it was the first time he had ever seen one. Then he looked from one to other of the children with admiration and gratitude.

'I think we'd better explain things to Tolly,' said Peter, at last. 'We're all getting too excited – and Tolly must be wondering what all that money is doing on the table! Even Scamper's excited! SIT, SCAMPER. Will you please SIT?'

'Well, young man – I can't say that I'm used to seeing so much money lying about,' said Tolly, with a wide grin. 'That twenty pound note looks as if it's just come straight from the Mint, it's so clean and new.'

'Anyway,' said George, proudly, 'it's for paying the vet's fees for Brownie. Or it *could* go towards buying him.'

'What's all this about buying him?' asked Tolly. 'I'm having ten pounds a week docked off my wages for five weeks – and then he'll be mine. I said Master Peter and Miss Janet here could share him, seeing that they live here, like, and can look after him sometimes. But he's *my* horse – *I'm* paying for him!'

'We thought that if you'd let us pay *part* of the money, we'd *really* feel he was partly ours. Which half of him shall we have?' Janet looked seriously at Tolly, and he laughed as he looked back at her.

'Now don't talk ridiculous, Miss,' he said. 'You can't buy a horse in two halves. We'll each share the whole of him, and I'll be pleased to think you've a share of his love. I never did see such a loving horse before. Why, I believe he'd work his heart out for his owners!'

'Well, Mr Tolly, listen,' said Peter. 'We shan't feel as if we're *really* sharing him if we don't pay part for him – all the club members think the same. We'd all like to feel that we've shares in such a lovely horse. But we know he's *really* yours! Just let's share him a *bit*!'

'Right,' said Tolly, understanding at last. Of course! None of these children actually had a horse of his or her own – and they longed to have even a small share in one. Tolly understood that. Yes, he understood that. He nodded his head and gave the children a wide grin.

'All right, Master Peter. That's settled then. Pay me twenty-five pence down, and you can reckon on your bit of him! And if you've any money left over, as I know you will have, then pay off a bit of the vet's fees – that would be right kind of you! I'll be a bit short for some weeks, paying over to the master for Brownie – and I can't manage the vet's fees too.'

'I tell you what!' said George. 'Let's pay half the vet's fees, and then just hand over what's left to Mr Tolly, to tide him over a bit. *We* don't want the money. The Secret Seven don't owe anything to anyone – and we can always earn a bit more if we want to by doing odd jobs for our parents. And there will be birthdays coming along soon.'

'I wonder when *Brownie's* birthday is,' said Pam. 'If we have any money left over we could buy him a whole bag of carrots. When's his birthday, do you know, Mr Tolly?'

'That's in about ten days' time,' said Tolly, screwing up his eyes as he tried to remember. 'I've got it written down somewhere, Missy. A bit of a thing he was – all legs and head – a bonny wee horse, though. Now look at him – as fine a horse as ever I did see!'

'I think we might as well go and visit the vet

today,' said Janet. 'We'd just have time to catch him before he goes out on his rounds. Shall we go?'

'Yes,' said Peter. 'We'll have time to go to his place, talk to him, and get back to finish our meeting. We'd better take the money with us. I do hope to goodness we've got enough. Come on, Scamper!'

They said goodbye to Tolly, and set off to the vet's house with Scamper trotting beside them. They were lucky. He was *just* going out after having seen his surgery patients, and was on his own fine horse.

'Hello, Mr Whistler,' said Peter, raising his cap. 'Can we speak to you just for a minute? You don't need to dismount, sir. My, isn't he a fine horse?'

'Yes. He's a grand fellow,' said the vet, patting the horse on his neck. 'His name's Lord Lofty – suits him, doesn't it?'

'Yes!' agreed the children, also patting the great horse. And Pam added, 'He *is* lordly – look at the way he holds his head aloft, and see how proudly he paws the ground. I'll bring you some sugar lumps next time I come, Lord Lofty, and kneel and present them to you on a silver plate!'

That made them all laugh. 'Well!' said the vet. 'Now what can I do for you? I'm just off on my rounds, and can only stop for a moment.'

'It's just that we've saved up the money to pay your bill for the horse called Brownie,' explained Peter. 'You know it, sir – Mr Dinneford had it – a lovely brown horse with a beautiful head. Mr Dinneford sold it to my father, and now my father has sold it to Tolly, who's left Mr Dinneford, and is now working for my father. Rather a long explanation, I'm afraid, sir.'

'Yes, yes. I know the horse well – he pulled a heavy cart downhill, and the cart pushed into his hind legs in some way, and injured them,' said the vet. 'I was angry with Dinneford over that – he always overworks his horses – uses two when he ought to use four! That horse suffered a lot – how are his legs now?'

'Well, sir, *we* think they are a lot better, now that Tolly's with us and looking after Brownie,' said Peter. 'And Tolly told us that you were a great help with old Brownie, and did a lot for him and his poor hurt legs. And, sir, we've come to pay the bill. You kindly said you would halve the fees, which is very good of you. So if you could tell us EXACTLY how much the bill is now, we thought we'd pay it, and then Tolly wouldn't worry about it any more. We've got enough money, sir. We've all saved up – and George here, he won twenty-five pounds in an essay competition.'

'And he gave it towards your fees, sir, and towards buying a share in Brownie. We're *all* going to share in Brownie,' said Colin, his face beaming. 'So he'll be jolly well looked after, sir.'

'Well, I'm blessed! So *that's* what you've come for!' said the vet, smiling. 'Let's see now – my bill was pretty high – and I said I'd halve it – now look, I suppose you wouldn't like *me* to have a share in that horse, would you? I'm fond of him too, you know – and if I had a share in him, I could come and look after him for nothing if anything went wrong, couldn't I?'

There was a silence, as the children worked out what this meant. '*Er* – well, sir,' said Peter. 'Of *course* you could have a share in him too. You must be fond of him, seeing you've done such a lot for his poor old back legs. Yes, I'm sure Tolly would like you to have a share in him. But about your bill, sir – if you could tell us what the half-payment is, we . . .'

'Good gracious – as if I should charge anything for looking after a horse in which *I* own a share!' said the vet, looking quite upset.

'But you *didn't* have a share when you attended him, sir,' said Colin.

'Quite right. But I didn't know then that I was

going to be lucky enough to be *allowed* a share in him, did I?' said the vet. 'No, no – you must let me have my way in this. Give me a share in the horse, and there'll be NO fees to pay for my attending Brownie when his legs were so bad. I wouldn't HEAR of it. Well, I must go. Goodbye – and pat Brownie for me, will you, and tell him that he's partly mine now, bless him!'

And with that the vet galloped off at top speed on Lord Lofty.

'WELL!' said Peter, jubilantly. 'That's that. What a wonderful thing to happen! Good old vet – he's a sport! And to think that if Brownie gets anything wrong with him, he'll get free treatment. No big bills for Tolly to worry about. Why, Pam – what's the matter? What on *earth* are you crying for?'

'It's only just because I'm so happy, all of a sudden,' wept Pam. 'I don't know *why* I'm crying. I just can't help it. I'm so surprised and happy. Don't look so worried, Scamper. I tell you I'm very *happy*!'

All right, Pam. Everyone understands! Quite a lot of people would do the same, if they came across such unexpected kindness!

Eleven

Everybody's pleased

THE children all went back to Peter's house as fast as ever they could. They could hardly believe their good luck! How kind of the vet! But how like him!

'I hope I'll be as generous as that when I grow up,' said George, solemnly. He had been very impressed with the vet's simple, heartfelt kindness. So money didn't count with some people, then? That was wonderful. Kindness mattered much more to the vet than even *pounds* of money. George never forgot that morning – and one day he was to grow up, and do the same kind of things – all because he talked to the vet about Brownie!

Tolly couldn't believe their good luck either, when they burst in on him as he sat having his mid-morning snack, in the little old shed near the stables.

They slapped all the money down on the bench beside him – the twenty pound note and the rest.

'The vet wouldn't take a penny!' said George.

'Not a penny. He said that all he wanted was a share in Brownie, he likes him so much and he'll come to see his legs for nothing! It's *true* Tolly!'

'You're having me on!' said Tolly, disbelievingly. 'That's what you're doing. Pulling my leg. Go on with you. You haven't been to the vet's! Have they, Scamper?'

It took some time to persuade Tolly that what they were telling him was the truth. Then he stood up, looking amazed. 'You mean to say that the vet didn't take a penny of your money?' he said. 'Not a penny? He's a gentleman, he is. A right-down, slap-up, true gentleman! And I'm going to take up to him all the eggs that my hen Sukey lays, every single one of them. He likes new-laid eggs – he told me he did. And he shall have Sukey's, if I go without eggs for the rest of my life.'

The children were amused by Tolly's outburst, and very pleased. Now the vet would have new-laid eggs every breakfast-time – and he certainly deserved them, everyone agreed on that.

'Funny how one kind deed leads to another, isn't it?' said Janet. 'Dear me – things have been very exciting lately. A bit *too* exciting. I feel quite out of breath. Oh well – I expect they'll quieten down now – but I must say I've enjoyed the last few days!'

Janet was wrong! They *didn't* quieten down! Instead they became very exciting indeed.

Peter went to tell his father what the vet had said, and Janet went with him. He listened without saying a word. Then when Peter came to the end of the story, he nodded his head.

'So he wouldn't take your money!' he said. 'Well, what are you going to do with it? It amounts to quite a bit.'

'We'd like to give it to you to pay for Brownie, so that Tolly can have him really and truly. He does so love him. Daddy – and after all, *he'll* be the one that has to look after him – we'll soon be back at school – and you're always busy. He'll be safe with Tolly and the other horses, won't he?'

'He'll be safe all right,' said Daddy. He gave them each a hug. 'Very well. I'll take the money, and it shall all be spent on Brownie – on his food, his stabling, and everything. And maybe there'll be enough to spend on a good saddle, so that you can ride him. He'd like that.'

'Oooh – so would *we*! said Janet, at once, her eyes bright. '*I* know, Daddy – let him be *your* horse and Tolly's when we're at school – and *our* horse when we're on holiday. That's fair enough, isn't it?'

'More than fair!' said Daddy. 'Now you go and

tell Mother all about this – I've some work to do out in the fields. I'll have a word with Tolly and tell him the arrangement we've made.'

'Well – that's fine!' said Peter, to Janet, as they went to tell their mother. 'I'll try to give Mother fifteen pence a week for a supply of sugar lumps for Brownie. He gets some from Tolly too, so he'll be well off. Isn't he a nice horse, Janet – and to think we can ride him every day!'

Tolly was as pleased as anyone else about the new arrangement. 'Do Brownie good to have someone to ride him every day,' he said. 'He'll get fat if he doesn't get plenty of exercise. His kind of horse runs to fat very quickly. You can jump him, too, you know. He's a good jumper. You should have seen him leaping over the stream yesterday when a dog came barking round his ankles. I vow the dog thought he had wings! Anyway, he took to his heels and fled, and old Brownie, he stood grinning there on the other side of the stream, showing all his beautiful white teeth. I guess that dog thought he was going to be eaten up, when he caught sight of those teeth!'

The children laughed. Old Tolly knew how to tell a story all right! They followed him into the stables and sat down in the sweetly-smelling hay.

'Tell us a story, Tolly,' said Janet. 'You know such a lot of tales about the animals you've worked with.'

'No, no – I'm busy now,' said Tolly. 'These stables have got to be mucked out. Look, you take that fork there, Master Peter, and give me a bit of help. You go and talk to old Brownie, Miss Janet. He's along there, and maybe he'd like an apple out of the loft. And maybe you would, too!'

Soon Janet was sitting in Brownie's part of the stable, each of them munching apples. The horse gave a gentle little whinny, and nosed at Janet lovingly. The girl put her arms round his neck and smelt his nice clean horse-smell.

'I do like you, Brownie,' she whispered in his pricked ear. 'You won't get stolen, will you? I couldn't bear it. I'll look out of the window tonight to make sure there are no thieves about. It will be a clear, moonlight night, and I can see your stables from my bedroom. So don't feel afraid – I shall be looking out to see you're in no danger – or the other horses either. I'll send Scamper out to you if I see any thieves!'

Twelve

In the middle of the night

EVERYONE went to bed early that night. Peter's father was tired for he had been helping with the farm-work, as one of the men was on holiday. Mother was always sleepy at night, and glad to go early. Only the children wanted to stay up to finish their books, but they were sent off to bed in spite of their complaints.

'And you're not to read in bed for hours and hours, see?' said Mother. 'You're to put out your lights in good time. Be good children, now.'

So off they went, grumbling. Their bedrooms were next to each other, so they could call to one another easily. They settled down with their books. Janet had a very, very exciting one, about smugglers' caves, and she read on and on, quite forgetting the time.

'You'll get a good scolding in the morning when you own up to the time you put out your light!' called Peter, putting his out. 'Good night, bookworm.'

Janet's book was certainly very exciting. She forgot all about the time. In fact, she forgot that she was in bed, she was so sure she was in the smugglers' caves with four children and their dog Timmy.

The clock downstairs struck very solemnly indeed. It was the big grandfather clock, and he had a deep, grave note. Janet listened, and counted. Good gracious – ELEVEN o'clock! Whatever would Mother say when she had to own up in the morning that she had heard old Grandfather strike eleven? Guiltily she put her book on the floor, put out her light, and drew back the curtain. At once the room was absolutely flooded in bright silver moonlight!

'How beautiful!' whispered Janet. 'Oh, how BEAUTIFUL! Just like extra lovely daylight with a sort of silver sheen.' She stood and looked out for a while, and then made up her mind.

I must go out in it, I must, I must! she thought. It's a fairy sort of night. I'll put on my dressing-gown and go and dance in the moonlight. I shan't tell anyone though – they'd think I was mad!

She pulled on her dressing-gown, called Scamper in a whisper from Peter's bedroom, and set off down the stairs. It all seemed very exciting, and not a bit frightening. The moonlight was so very, *very* bright!

She went out of the back door, and stood in the yard gazing up at the moon sailing along in the sky. It looked very big indeed.

I *can't* go back to bed when the moon is shining so beautifully! thought Janet. I know! I'll go and see if Brownie is awake! I'll whisper in his ear and tell him I've come to see him, because the moonlight is so bright. He'll be so pleased to see me.

She was afraid to walk round the yard in the moonlight just in *case* her mother or father happened to be awake and standing at the window to look at the moon. So she went quietly all round the yard in the shadows, Scamper close beside her.

And then Scamper suddenly gave a growl and stopped. He pulled at Janet's night-dress and gave another little growl. She stopped absolutely still in the dark shadow of a tree, and listened. What was Scamper growling at? A rat? A mouse running into its hole? She could hear no sound at all, and see no mouse or rat. So on she went again, still keeping in the shadows.

And then she heard a noise. It sounded like an exclamation – somewhere in the stables. Who could be there? Well, Tolly, of course. He always bedded down in straw or hay in the stables, his old mattress beneath him. He couldn't bear to leave his beloved horses!

Janet's heart began to beat very loudly indeed, and very fast. She put her hand on Scamper's collar, and whispered in his ear. 'Don't bark or growl. Keep close to me. I'll find out what's going on. I'll peep in at one of the stable windows. Now be quiet, Scamper, be quiet!'

Together they kept in the shadows and came to the big stables. The horses were restless, and were

stamping their feet and moving about. One gave a little whinny.

And then a great noise sprang up! At least, it seemed a great noise to Janet, crouching in the shadows! There were shouts – yes, shouts in Tolly's voice. There were excited whinnies. There was the sound of men's feet. Then Tolly's voice came, 'HELP! HELP!'

Janet could now see into one of the stable windows. She looked down into the stables, and saw a fight going on. There were three men there, one holding Brownie, one holding another horse, and the third fighting poor Tolly! Crack! Bang! Biff! What a fight. Janet was terrified and couldn't help giving a scream. Tolly heard her, but the others didn't. He called out to the frightened girl peeping down at the fight from the window just above him. 'Get help quickly! Save the horses!'

'No good calling for help, old man!' said one of the thieves, roughly. 'There's no one near these stables!'

Janet, really frightened, raced back to the house in her dressing-gown and slippers. 'DADDY! MUMMY! Quick, the horse-thieves are there! Tolly's fighting them! Daddy, DADDY!'

Her father and mother awoke at once, and her

father raced downstairs in his pyjamas. When Janet ran into the house, her mother was already telephoning the police!

She sobbed out about Tolly being attacked, and her mother comforted her. 'The police will be here in a minute,' she said. 'You go into the drive and wait for them, and take them to the stables. I must go and see if I can help your father!' And, taking a large kitchen poker with her, she fled outside in her dressing-gown. How brave! thought Janet, proudly, waiting in the drive. Oh dear – why doesn't Peter wake up!

Just then the police drove up in their car. 'Hey, Miss – where's the fuss? Quick, tell us!' called a voice, and a big, strong policeman ran up to her.

'I'll take you,' cried Janet. 'Someone's stealing our horses. I saw them. Daddy's gone to stop them and Mother's gone too.'

What with shouts and yells, and whinnies and barks, a tremendous noise was coming from the stables! Janet began to tremble, but she bravely trailed behind the police in her old dressing-gown! Were her mother and father all right? What had happened to Tolly? Were the horses hurt – or Scamper?

She didn't want to go to the stables to see what

was happening, but she had to. Good gracious, what a turmoil!

There was Daddy firmly on top of one horse-thief. And there was Tolly on top of another, hitting him well and truly. And dear me, there was a third one, down on his knees in front of Mother, begging her to let him go!

Codger and Scamper were having a simply wonderful time. They kept darting at the men and snapping at them, and the men were scared stiff. All the horses were upset and excited, scuffling and stamping and whinnying in their stalls. Janet felt as if she simply must sit down. Everything was *much* too exciting. So she sat on the cold stone wall outside the stables and waited for the fight to die down. Good gracious – WHAT a thing to happen! Oh, poor Peter – he was in bed, out of all this excitement. She really, really, must fetch him!

Thirteen

What an excitement!

JANET decided to go and get Peter before all the excitement was over. He'd never, never forgive her if she didn't. So she flew upstairs at top speed, and shook him awake. 'Peter! Come quickly! We've got horse-thieves in the stable! Tolly fought them, and now the police are here and Daddy and Mother and everybody's fighting in the stables!'

'Don't be silly! You've just had a bad dream!' said Peter, astonished and cross. 'Go back to bed. Fancy waking me with a silly story like *that*!' And he turned over to go to sleep again. Janet shook him hard.

'Sit up, sit up!' she shouted. 'Then you can hear the row. You'll miss all the excitement. Anyway. I'm going to watch from the window!'

By this time Peter began to think there might be something in what Janet was shouting about. So he leapt out of bed and ran to the window with her. Good gracious! What a row – what shouts – what biffs and scuffles – what barks from Scamper and excited neighs from the horses!

'Come on!' said Peter, and without waiting to put on his dressing-gown or slippers he fled downstairs, out into the yard, and into the stable. Whew, *what* an excitement!

Most of the trouble was over now. But what a fight it had been! Tolly had gone for the thieves with a pitchfork, and made them dance in pain. They had tried to let out the horses, but the brave beasts had stood their ground, and Brownie had done quite a bit of snapping and kicking. The men were terrified of him. He had got one of them into a corner, and the man did not dare to move, and was glad when a sturdy policeman came up to handcuff him! 'Take that horse away from me,' begged the man. 'He's just about broken my ankle with a kick, and I wouldn't be surprised if he's bitten my ear off.'

'I hope he *has*,' said the policeman, grimly, and pushed the man roughly into the next stall, where two other men had also been imprisoned. One had been kicked on the arm, and was nursing the wounded limb, his face angry and fierce. The third man had been knocked down when Tolly had flung himself on him, and had a badly cut head.

'Are the horses hurt?' Janet asked Tolly, who,

breathless with the fight, was standing holding on to one of the thieves.

'No, Miss – not hurt at all,' panted Tolly. 'Old Brownie's enjoyed the shindy. My, my – the way he pranced about, and kicked out with those big hooves of his! I began to feel sorry for these horse-thieves! I was knocked down once, but old Brownie came up and almost snapped the man's arm off. Good old Brownie. He wasn't a bit afraid, Miss. He was clever too. He never so much as snapped at a policeman – only at the thieves!'

With a lot of shoving and pushing the horse-thieves were taken to the police cars. They were difficult to handle, and, to Peter's delight, he saw that every thief had a good stout policeman sitting down hard on him. There certainly would be no escape for *them*!

'Everything seems very quiet suddenly,' said Mother. 'My word, what an adventure! What a good thing you were awake, Janet, and heard the thieves.'

'Er – well, actually I was still reading,' confessed Janet. 'And the moonlight was so lovely I decided to go out in it with Scamper – and heard the noise in the stables. Are you hurt, Tolly? Fancy – you *thought* horse-thieves might be coming some night,

and you were right. What a good thing you sleep with the horses!'

'I wouldn't sleep anywhere else if I knew horse-thieves were about!' said Tolly, brushing himself down.

The horses were restive and uneasy. 'I think, sir, if it's all right with you I'll take them all out for a quiet canter,' said Tolly. Then they'll probably settle down quietly for the rest of the night.'

'Right, Tolly. And thanks for all your help tonight,' said Peter's father. 'I'll see you get some reward for it. It's good to have a man like you on the job.'

'Tolly – what exactly happened?' asked Janet, excitedly.

'Well, Miss, I bedded down in the straw on my old mattress, in the stall next to old Brownie, see? And the horses, they went to sleep, seemingly, because I didn't hear much stamping or whinnying. And then, some time later on, old Brownie here he whinnied right in my ear – leaned over my stall and whinnied, he did. Quiet-like, as if he wanted to whisper.

'Well, I sat up, of course, and there he was looking down at me anxious-like. The moonlight was shining into the stable and it was as bright as day, Miss. Then I heard another noise – and that wasn't a noise made by any horse, Miss. It was a man sneezing, and trying to stop his sneeze. And I thought to myself, Oho, Here we go! Horse-thieves, or I'll eat my old cap!'

'What then?' asked Janet, breathlessly, her heart still beating fast.

'Well, then up I gets, pushes open the half-door, and stands up to see what was what. And I saw a man undoing the latch of Major's stall, up there, see. And old Major he began to carry on alarming. He snorted and whinnied and stamped till I thought he'd bring the stable down. How that man got him out of his stall, I don't know – but I do know that as soon as Major had room to kick out, he did – and that fellow went flying from one end of the stable to the other! Then I saw more chaps and I went mad. I picked up that there pitchfork and they struggled with me like madmen. They didn't want to get pricked by that sharp old fork. But there's one of them won't be able to sit down for a fortnight, that he won't!'

And old Tolly went off into a hoot of laughter that made all the horses turn round and look at him.

'Go on, Tolly. This is a tale worth telling,' said Peter's father, looking grim and amused at one and the same time.

'I don't rightly know what I did next,' said Tolly, scratching his head. 'I do know I saw one of them with my old Brownie again, and I caught hold of Brownie's head, swung him round and told him to kick the fellows out – send them flying. And old Brownie, he's always obedient, you know. My word, he sent two of them flying! One cracked his head on a door – and didn't he howl! "Shame on you," I said, "you'll wake up all the bobbies in the district" – and bless me, sir, at that very minute the police came and joined the fight. Like magic, it was!'

'Well, you've done a grand and a brave job tonight, Tolly,' said Peter's father. 'I hope you'll regard yourself as on my permanent staff now – head of the stables – and over any of the younger staff. I can do with a man like you here! Why that fellow Dinneford let you go, I don't know! Well – see to the horses for a while and quieten them and then bed down yourself. Good night.'

And with that he put his arm round his wife's shoulders, motioned to the two excited children to go on in front and shepherded everyone back inside the house, including a most excited Scamper.

'How any of us are going to sleep tonight, I don't know!' he said. 'Too exciting for words! Well – we'll talk about it in the morning – and now – good night, Peter, good night, Janet. Sleep well!'

The children didn't want to go back to bed. They wanted to stay and talk and talk about all that had happened. They wanted to go and speak to each of the horses, they wanted to talk to Tolly – in fact, they wanted to do anything but go to bed.

But their father was determined. 'I said "Go back to bed" and I meant it. You'll catch frightful colds staying out here with so little on, after being in warm beds – and you're missing your night's sleep. If you don't go back to bed straight away now I shall forbid you to go near Tolly *or* the stables tomorrow, and that you won't like at all!'

'All right, Daddy – we're going,' grinned Peter. 'Goodness, what a night! I've never had an adventure like *this* before – in our very own home. What in the world will the other members of the Secret Seven say when we tell them tomorrow!'

'Off you go, for the last time!' said his father, giving him a firm push. 'Go and think about it in bed.'

At last the two children were safely in bed, shouting remarks to one another from their different rooms. Then suddenly Peter had no answer to his questions and knew that Janet was asleep!

Both children slept late when morning came, and didn't even hear the breakfast gong. Their mother let them lie in bed, remembering how late they had been the night before. But they were cross when they got up at last and found that quite a bit of the morning had gone. 'Oh, *Mother*! We wanted to go round and call the Secret Seven to another meeting!' grumbled Peter. 'They *must* know all that happened last night. It was so very, very exciting.'

'Will you please finish your breakfast and stop grumbling, Peter dear?' said his mother. 'You've the whole day to call a meeting. I shall clear away your breakfast in exactly ten minutes' time, so if you *want* a good breakfast you'd better get on with it.'

It was exciting to talk about the night before. Immediately breakfast was over they went to talk to Tolly. He was rubbing down one of the horses, whistling between his teeth. He grinned at the two children.

'Well – we had a night of it, didn't we?' he said. 'They nearly got my old Brownie! Ah, they didn't know how loudly he could hrrrrrrrrumph! Woke me up at once, he did.'

'They didn't know that you slept in the stable with the horses, either, else they'd have been more careful,' said Janet. 'You're very fierce, aren't you,

Tolly? I felt quite scared of you last night when I saw you with that hay fork.'

'I reckon *they* feel scared of me this morning too,' said Tolly, wringing out his cloth in the horse-pail. 'I keep thinking of that chap that won't be able to sit down for a week – and the other one, *he* won't be able to walk for a fortnight!'

'A jolly good thing too!' said Peter.

'Well, it's what horse-thieves deserve!' said old Tolly. 'I remember the last time I had to do with a horse-thief. He came stealing past my cottage into the stables I was in at that time, and I saw his shadow on my blind. Well, me and Codger, we got up at once, and I took my old pail with me – and I told Codger to chase the man to the old pump – and my, when I got there too, I worked the pump and filled my pail, and over the fellow's head went the icy-cold water. He couldn't get away – Codger saw to that – and I threw five more pails of water over him. Laugh! I had to sit down on the old wall to get my breath, I'd such a stitch in my side.'

Tolly knew how to tell a story very well, and the children could have listened for ages. But Tolly had work to do.

'Wait a minute, Tolly, wait,' said Peter. 'We're going to spend some of that money on a birthday party for Brownie, and all of us – you too – are to come. We'll get some very special oats for Brownie, and a whole pound of sugar lumps and . . .'

'Now look here, Master Peter, nobody's going to give my Brownie a pound of sugar lumps!' said Tolly, in alarm. 'He'd be as fat as an old cow in no time – and his poor back legs would have even more weight to carry. He . . .'

'It's all right, Tolly. We shall give *you* the sugar lumps to dole out to him!' said Peter. 'Or you can dole them out to us to give him. We promise not to make him fat. He's exactly right as he is!'

No notes needed to be written to call the Secret Seven to a meeting. When the news ran round Peterswood that horse-thieves had been to Peter's house, the rest of the members came rushing down to find out what had happened! Peter took them all down to the little meeting-shed.

The members sat down expectantly, all agog to hear everything. 'The milkman told *me*,' said Pam. 'And I rushed round and told the others – but most of them knew, Peter, what happened? Are the horses safe?'

'Perfectly,' said Peter. 'But I have a fresh piece of news for everyone. The night before they came to us, they went to Mr Dinneford's – and took his three *best* horses! And nobody knows where they are yet.'

'Serve him right,' said George, and the others nodded in agreement. 'Horrid man! Well, he lost Tolly through his bad temper and meanness – and now he's lost three of his horses. Will the horses be all right?'

'Oh yes – they are too valuable to be ill-treated by the thieves – they'll be all right except for a fright. But goodness knows where the thieves have taken them to – or who has bought them!'

'Well – I just *can't* feel sorry for Mr Dinneford,' said Peter. 'When I think how he spoilt dear old Brownie's hind legs through making him work with an overloaded cart, I just think to myself, "Well, serve him right!"'

'I think we all feel like that,' said Barbara. 'Peter, did you find out when Brownie's birthday is?'

'Oh yes – that's really what I wanted to call a meeting about,' said Peter. 'It's on Friday. I've spoken to Dad about it, and he says he'd like to join in too, and make it a really good day for Brownie and Tolly. Don't you think we ought to ask Bob too? It was he who told us about Brownie and Tolly.'

'Yes – of course ask him – fine!' said George, and the others nodded in complete agreement.

'Dad says that he thinks it would be a good idea to spend most of the money we have left on helping to buy a decent saddle for Brownie,' said Peter. 'Then Tolly can ride him in comfort, and Brownie will love that. Dad also said that we must get a really good one, and so *he* will put some money towards the saddle too, as he feels so grateful to Tolly for saving our horses last night.'

'Good idea!' cried everyone, very pleased, and Colin added, 'Your father is great!'

'Well, there'll be plenty of money left for a super party,' said Peter. 'I vote we have it in the stable yard, so that all the horses can look out of the stable – and see us – and we can give them sugar lumps so that they can feel they're in the party too.'

'Hurray!' cheered everyone, getting really excited. 'Hurray!'

And that is why they are now all sitting down to a long table set out in the stable yard. Brownie's birthday has arrived. He is thirteen years old today, though he doesn't know it. He can't *imagine* why everyone is making such a fuss of him – and look at the garland of flowers he's wearing – doesn't he look fine! Dear old Brownie – everyone loves you!

Hanging in the stable is a fine new saddle, just right for Brownie to wear. That's what Peter's

father and the children bought for Tolly – and he's so proud of it that he can hardly wait to put it on Brownie's back and ride him.

There's a birthday cake too, with 'Happy Birthday, Brownie!' on it. Well, well – if ever a horse could be proud, Brownie could be today!

But he's not at all conceited. There he stands, look, his big brown eyes as kind as ever, his coat shining beautifully. Ah – sugar lumps! Good! And a slice of iced cake – even better! And a fine handful of the very best corn from Tolly's horny hand – a very nice titbit indeed.

'Hrrrumph, hrrrumph, hrrrumph!' says Brownie, and everyone laughs as Brownie nods his head politely.

'He says "Thanks, thanks, thanks!"' says Janet. 'Mr Tolly – I really do think he's the nicest horse in the world!'

'You're right there, Missy you're right!' said Tolly, taking Brownie another piece of cake, and look, Brownie is nuzzling into his ear, just as if he is whispering to the old man.

'He says he reckons there's no children like *you*!' reported Tolly, and that made everyone laugh.

Well, I think Brownie's right, Secret Seven. I really do think he's right!